THE JAZZ AGE

Bibelot

F. SCOTT FITZGERALD

THE JAZZ AGE

INTRODUCTION BY E.L. DOCTOROW

A NEW DIRECTIONS

Manufactured in the United States of America
New Directions Books are printed on acid-free paper.
First published as a New Directions Bibelot in 1996
Published simultaneously in Canada by Penguin Books Canada
Limited

Publisher's Note: The essays included in *The Jazz Age* were selected
from the New Directions edition of *The Crack-Up,* published originally clothbound in 1945, and as New Directions Paperbook 54 in 1956;
reissued as New Directions Paperbook 757 in 1993.

Library of Congress Cataloging-in-Publication Data

Fitzgerald, F. Scott (Francis Scott), 1896-1940
    The jazz age / F. Scott Fitzgerald ; introduction by E.L. Doctorow
    p.   cm.
    "A New Directions bibelot."
    ISBN 0-8112-1333-1
    I. Title.
PS3511.I9J39   1996
813' .52–dc20   96-23031
                                     CIP

Celebrating 60 years of publishing for James Laughlin
by New Directions Publishing Corporation,
80 Eighth Avenue New York 10011

THIRD PRINTING

CONTENTS

INTRODUCTION

E.L. DOCTOROW

Of that triumvirate of hero-novelists who came of age
in the 1920's, we may salute the big two-hearted
pugilist, and stand in awe of the mesmerist from
Mississippi, but it's the third one we mourn, the Jazz
Age kid, our own Fitzgerald. His was the most natural
and unforced of the three authorial voices; his plots
required minimal invention; his settings were for the
most part the surroundings of his readers. All of that
was working the high wire without a net. He lived rash-
ly, susceptible to the worst influences of his time, and
lacking any defense against stronger personalities than
his own; and when he died, at forty-four, he was gener-
ally recognized to have abused his genius as badly as he
had his constitution. Yet at his best, in *The Great
Gatsby*, much of *Tender Is the Night*, and the incom-
plete *Last Tycoon*, he wrote nearer to the societal heart
than either of his august contemporaries.

The Fitzgerald of these autobiographical pieces is
the chastened, mature man, sober, alone, with nothing
to lose. He is writing in the Great Depression, but ignor-
ing it except as the turn of events which has, not without justice, dropped him and his jazz-age ways into the
dustbin of history. In a time of breadlines and hobo
jungles, and with totalitarian states rising all over
Europe, somehow the young man who, one drunken

night, leapt into the fountain at the Plaza, can not expect, still, to be everyone's idea of the great American author. But he can reminisce. He can remember the Twenties—he can look back on his early success, or the New York of his youthful illusions, or his and his wife's years of sybaritic hotel hoppings, or the circumstances leading to his nervous collapse—and he can render them, bring them back alive for our consideration. Not surprisingly, his tone is elegiac, the sense of a paradise lost infuses every line. But rarely is there a lapse into self-pity. And underneath all is the shrewd writer's assessment of his own rise and fall as a saleable subject. The unstated presumption in *The Crack-Up* (originally published in three installments in *Esquire*) is the author's still lingering celebrity: that golden boy you all remember—see what's become of him.

Whether writing about himself or the changing manners and morals and social dynamics of the time that made him its symbol, Fitzgerald writes with clinical precision. At moments a poetic fever may take hold, when his metaphors stumble over one another in his determination to get through to his magazine audience, but he consistently offers the insights of a first rate cultural historian. And whatever we say in criticism of him, we find that he has said it first. He is disarmingly confessional about his lack of sustained interest in the universal political crisis of his time, about the squandering of his literary capital in magazine hack work, about his life as a drunk, about his pathetic need always to prove something to somebody, about his snobberies and prejudices, all held with the passion of an *arriviste*. Everything we know about him, he knows about himself. And it turns out that all along, through all the good times, he was haunted by his inauthenticity— as the young Lieutenant in his World War I overseas cap who never got overseas, as well as the urbane young Author carried on the shoulders of his generation, "who knew less of New York than any reporter of six months standing, and less of its society than any hall-room boy in a Ritz stag line."

Repeatedly he disclaims his role as spokesman and symbol of the Jazz Age, but by reflecting upon it from his chosen distance, he tolls its dreadful excesses in his own life, and so finds its meaning in the body of his wrecked career. There is gallantry in that. We begin to understand our particular affection for this writer. He lacked armor. He did not live in protective seclusion, as Faulkner. He was not carapaced in self-presentation, as Hemingway. He jumped right into the foolish heart of everything, as he had into the Plaza fountain. He was intellectually ambitious—but thought fashion was important, gossip, good looks, the company of celebrities. He wrote as a rebel, a sophisticate, an escapee from American provincialism—but was blown away by society like a country bumpkin, and went everywhere he was invited. Ambivalently willed, he lived as both particle and wave. "The test of a first-rate intelligence," he wrote, "is the ability to hold two opposed ideas in the mind at the same time, and still retain the ability to function." And while he was at his first rate quantum best, he used everything he knew of society, as critic, as victim, to compose at least one work, *The Great Gatsby*, that in its few pages arcs the American continent and gives us a perfect structural allegory of our deadly class-ridden longings.

The contemporary reader may have to work to understand the nature of the celebrated crack-up. Fitzgerald tells us that his "nervous reflexes were giving way—too much anger and too many tears." What condition is he describing? A psychotic episode? Depression? A spiritual crisis? There is a muttering resolve in his account of it, a determination at the end to change, to be available no longer to the humiliations that have characterized his fate. "Cave canem," he warns those of us who would come importuning to his door. We have to smile in our sadness for our greying Jazz-Age kid. Such bitter resolution is not characteristic of the psychological breakdown, the depleted vitality of the depressive. It is more the angry Romantic's expression of inconsolability—in having had an innocence and, having lost it, having to mourn it. That progression of states of the American mind was prevalent once upon a time, but now, at the end of this century of industrialized war and genocide, is itself to be mourned.

THE JAZZ AGE

Bibelot

ECHOES OF THE JAZZ AGE

ECHOES OF THE
JAZZ AGE

November, 1931

IT is too soon to write about the Jazz Age with perspective, and without being suspected of premature arteriosclerosis. Many people still succumb to violent retching when they happen upon any of its characteristic words—words which have since yielded in vividness to the coinages of the under-world. It is as dead as were the Yellow Nineties in 1902. Yet the present writer already looks back to it with nostalgia. It bore him up, flattered him and gave him more money than he had dreamed of, simply for telling people that he felt as they did, that something had to be done with all the nervous energy stored up and unexpended in the War.

The ten-year period that, as if reluctant to die outmoded in its bed, leaped to a spectacular death in October, 1929, began about the time of the May Day riots in 1919. When the police rode down the demobilized country boys gaping at the orators in Madison Square, it was the sort of measure bound to alienate the more intelligent young men from the prevailing order. We didn't remember anything about the

3

Bill of Rights until Mencken began plugging it, but we did know that such tyranny belonged in the jittery little countries of South Europe. If goose-livered business men had this effect on the government, then maybe we had gone to war for J. P. Morgan's loans after all. But, because we were tired of Great Causes, there was no more than a short outbreak of moral indignation, typified by Dos Passos' *Three Soldiers*. Presently we began to have slices of the national cake and our idealism only flared up when the newspapers made melodrama out of such stories as Harding and the Ohio Gang or Sacco and Vanzetti. The events of 1919 left us cynical rather than revolutionary, in spite of the fact that now we are all rummaging around in our trunks wondering where in hell we left the liberty cap—"I know I *had* it"— and the moujik blouse. It was characteristic of the Jazz Age that it had no interest in politics at all.

It was an age of miracles, it was an age of art, it was an age of excess, and it was an age of satire. A Stuffed Shirt, squirming to blackmail in a lifelike way, sat upon the throne of the United States; a stylish young man hurried over to represent to us the throne of England. A world of girls yearned for the young Englishman; the old American groaned in his sleep as he waited to be poisoned by his wife, upon the advice of the female Rasputin who then made the ultimate decision in our national affairs. But such matters apart, we had things our way at last. With Americans ordering suits by the gross in London, the Bond Street tailors perforce agreed to moderate their cut to the American long-waisted figure and loose-fitting taste, something subtle passed to America, the style of man. During the Renaissance, Francis the First looked to Florence to trim his leg. Seven-

4

teenth-century England aped the court of France, and fift years ago the German Guards officer bought his civilian clothes in London. Gentlemen's clothes—symbol of "the power that man must hold and that passes from race to race."

We were the most powerful nation. Who could tell us any longer what was fashionable and what was fun? Isolated during the European War, we had begun combing the unknown South and West for folkways and pastimes, and there were more ready to hand.

The first social revelation created a sensation out of all proportion to its novelty. As far back as 1915 the unchaperoned young people of the smaller cities had discovered the mobile privacy of that automobile given to young Bill at sixteen to make him "self-reliant." At first petting was a desperate adventure even under such favorable conditions, but presently confidences were exchanged and the old commandment broke down. As early as 1917 there were references to such sweet and casual dalliance in any number of the *Yale Record* or the *Princeton Tiger*.

But petting in its more audacious manifestations was confined to the wealthier classes—among other young people the old standard prevailed until after the War, and a kiss meant that a proposal was expected, as young officers in strange cities sometimes discovered to their dismay. Only in 1920 did the veil finally fall—the Jazz Age was in flower.

Scarcely had the staider citizens of the republic caught their breaths when the wildest of all generations, the generation which had been adolescent during the confusion of the War, brusquely shouldered my contemporaries out of the way and danced into the limelight. This was the generation whose girls dramatized themselves as flappers, the generation that corrupted its elders and eventually overreached

5

ck of morals than through lack of taste.
xhibit the year 1922! That was the peak
generation, for though the Jazz Age con-
ame less and less an affair of youth.

quel was like a children's party taken over by the
, leaving the children puzzled and rather neglected
d rather taken aback. By 1923 their elders, tired of watching the carnival with ill-concealed envy, had discovered that young liquor will take the place of young blood, and with a whoop the orgy began. The younger generation was starred no longer.

A whole race going hedonistic, deciding on pleasure. The precocious intimacies of the younger generation would have come about with or without prohibition—they were implicit in the attempt to adapt English customs to American conditions. (Our South, for example, is tropical and early maturing—it has never been part of the wisdom of France and Spain to let young girls go unchaperoned at sixteen and seventeen.) But the general decision to be amused that began with the cocktail parties of 1921 had more complicated origins.

The word jazz in its progress toward respectability has meant first sex, then dancing, then music. It is associated with a state of nervous stimulation, not unlike that of big cities behind the lines of a war. To many English the War still goes on because all the forces that menace them are still active—Wherefore eat, drink and be merry, for to-morrow we die. But different causes had now brought about a corresponding state in America—though there were entire classes (people over fifty, for example) who spent a whole decade denying its existence even when its puckish face peered into the family circle. Never did they dream that they had contributed to it. The honest citizens of every class, who believed in a strict public morality and were powerful enough to enforce the necessary legislation, did not know that they would necessarily be served by criminals and quacks, and do not really believe it to-day. Rich righteousness had always been able to buy honest and intelligent servants to free the slaves or the Cubans, so when this attempt collapsed our elders stood firm with all the stubbornness of people involved in a weak case, preserving their righteousness and losing their children. Silver-haired women and men with fine old faces, people who never did a consciously dishonest thing in their lives, still assure each other in the apartment hotels of New York and Boston and Washington that "there's a whole generation growing up that will never know the taste of liquor." Meanwhile their granddaughters pass the well-thumbed copy of *Lady Chatterley's Lover* around the boarding-school and, if they get about at all, know the taste of gin or corn at sixteen. But the generation who reached maturity between 1875 and 1895 continue to believe what they want to believe.

Even the intervening generations were incredulous. In 1920 Heywood Broun announced that all this hubbub was nonsense, that young men didn't kiss but told anyhow. But very shortly people over twenty-five came in for an intensive education. Let me trace some of the revelations vouchsafed them by reference to a dozen works written for various types of mentality during the decade. We begin with the suggestion that Don Juan leads an interesting life (*Jurgen*, 1919); then we learn that there's a lot of sex around if we only knew it (*Winesburg, Ohio*, 1920) that adolescents lead very amorous lives (*This Side of Paradise*, 1920), that there are a lot of neglected Anglo-Saxon words (*Ulysses*, 1921), that older people don't always resist sudden temptations (*Cytherea*, 1922), that girls are sometimes seduced without being ruined (*Flaming Youth*, 1922), that even rape often turns out well (*The Sheik*, 1922), that glamorous English ladies are often promiscuous (*The Green Hat*, 1924), that in fact they devote most of their time to it (*The Vortex*, 1926), that it's a damn good thing too (*Lady Chatterley's Lover*, 1928), and finally that there are abnormal variations (*The Well of Loneliness*, 1928, and *Sodom and Gomorrah*, 1929).

In my opinion the erotic element in these works, even *The Sheik* written for children in the key of *Peter Rabbit*, did not one particle of harm. Everything they described, and much more, was familiar in our contemporary life. The majority of the theses were honest and elucidating—their effect was to restore some dignity to the male as opposed to the he-man in American life. ("And what is a 'He-man'?" demanded Gertrude Stein one day. "Isn't it a large enough order to fill out to the dimensions of all that 'a man' has meant in the past? A '*He*-man'!") The married woman can now discover whether she is being cheated, or whether sex is just something to be endured, and her compensation should be to establish a tyranny of the spirit, as her mother may have hinted. Perhaps many women found that love was meant to be fun. Anyhow the objectors lost their tawdry little case, which is one reason why our literature is now the most living in the world.

Contrary to popular opinion, the movies of the Jazz Age had no effect upon its morals. The social attitude of the producers was timid, behind the times and banal—for example, no picture mirrored even faintly the younger generation until 1923, when magazines had already been started to celebrate it and it had long ceased to be news.

There were a few feeble splutters and then Clara Bow in *Flaming Youth;* promptly the Hollywood hacks ran the theme into its cinematographic grave. Throughout the Jazz Age the movies got no farther than Mrs. Jiggs, keeping up with its most blatant superficialities. This was no doubt due to the censorship as well as to innate conditions in the industry. In any case, the Jazz Age now raced along under its own power, served by great filling stations full of money.

The people over thirty, the people all the way up to fifty, had joined the dance. We graybeards (to tread down F. P. A.) remember the uproar when in 1912 grandmothers of forty tossed away their crutches and took lessons in the Tango and the Castle-Walk. A dozen years later a woman might pack the Green Hat with her other affairs as she set off for Europe or New York, but Savonarola was too busy flogging dead horses in Augean stables of his own creation to notice. Society, even in small cities, now dined in separate chambers, and the sober table learned about the gay table only from hearsay. There were very few people left at the sober table. One of its former glories, the less sought-after girls who had become resigned to sublimating a probable celibacy, came across Freud and Jung in seeking their intellectual recompense and came tearing back into the fray.

By 1926 the universal preoccupation with sex had become a nuisance. (I remember a perfectly mated, contented young mother asking my wife's advice about "having an affair right away," though she had no one especially in mind, "because don't you think it's sort of undignified when you get much over thirty?") For a while bootleg Negro records with their phallic euphemisms made everything suggestive, and simultaneously came a wave of erotic plays—young girls from finishing-schools packed the galleries to hear about the romance of being a Lesbian and George Jean Nathan protested. Then one young producer lost his head entirely, drank a beauty's alcoholic bath-water and went to the penitentiary. Somehow his pathetic attempt at romance belongs to the Jazz Age, while his contemporary in prison, Ruth Snyder, had to be hoisted into it by the tabloids— she was, as *The Daily News* hinted deliciously to gourmets, about "to cook, *and sizzle, AND FRY!*" in the electric chair.

The gay elements of society had divided into two main streams, one flowing toward Palm Beach and Deauville, and the other, much smaller, toward the summer Riviera. One could get away with more on the summer Riviera, and whatever happened seemed to have something to do with art. From 1926 to 1929, the great years of the Cap d'Antibes, this corner of France was dominated by a group quite distinct from that American society which is dominated by Europeans. Pretty much of anything went at Antibes—by 1929, at the most gorgeous paradise for swimmers on the Mediterranean no one swam any more, save for a short hang-over dip at noon. There was a picturesque graduation of steep rocks over the sea and somebody's valet and an occasional English girl used to dive from them, but the Americans were content to discuss each other in the bar. This was indicative of something that was taking place in the homeland—Americans were getting soft. There were signs everywhere: we still won the Olympic games but with champions whose names had few vowels in them—teams composed, like the fighting Irish combination of Notre Dame, of fresh overseas blood. Once the French became really interested, the Davis Cup gravitated automatically to their intensity in competition. The vacant lots of the Middle-

Western cities were built up now—except for a short period in school, we were not turning out to be an athletic people like the British, after all. The hare and the tortoise. Of course if we wanted to we could be in a minute; we still had all those reserves of ancestral vitality, but one day in 1926 we looked down and found we had flabby arms and a fat pot and couldn't say boop-boop-a-doop to a Sicilian. Shades of Van Bibber!—no utopian ideal, God knows. Even golf, once considered an effeminate game, had seemed very strenuous of late—an emasculated form appeared and proved just right.

By 1927 a wide-spread neurosis began to be evident, faintly signalled, like a nervous beating of the feet, by the popularity of cross-word puzzles. I remember a fellow ex-patriate opening a letter from a mutual friend of ours, urging him to come home and be revitalized by the hardy, bracing qualities of the native soil. It was a strong letter and it affected us both deeply, until we noticed that it was headed from a nerve sanitarium in Pennsylvania.

By this time contemporaries of mine had begun to disappear into the dark maw of violence. A classmate killed his wife and himself on Long Island, another tumbled "accidently" from a skyscraper in Philadelphia, another purposely from a skyscraper in New York. One was killed in a speak-easy in Chicago; another was beaten to death in a speak-easy in New York and crawled home to the Princeton Club to die; still another had his skull crushed by a maniac's axe in an insane asylum where he was confined. These are not catastrophes that I went out of my way to look for— these were my friends; moreover, these things happened not during the depression but during the boom.

In the spring of '27, something bright and alien flashed

across the sky. A young Minnesotan who seemed to have had nothing to do with his generation did a heroic thing, and for a moment people set down their glasses in country clubs and speakeasies and thought of their old best dreams. Maybe there was a way out by flying, maybe our restless blood could find frontiers in the illimitable air. But by that time we were all pretty well committed; and the Jazz Age continued; we would all have one more.

Nevertheless, Americans were wandering ever more widely—friends seemed eternally bound for Russia, Persia, Abyssinia and Central Africa. And by 1928 Paris had grown suffocating. With each new shipment of Americans spewed up by the boom the quality fell off, until toward the end there was something sinister about the crazy boatloads. They were no longer the simple pa and ma and son and daughter, infinitely superior in their qualities of kindness and curiosity to the corresponding class in Europe, but fantastic neanderthals who believed something, something vague, that you remembered from a very cheap novel. I remember an Italian on a steamer who promenaded the deck in an American Reserve Officer's uniform picking quarrels in broken English with Americans who criticised their own institutions in the bar. I remember a fat Jewess, inlaid with diamonds, who sat behind us at the Russian ballet and said as the curtain rose, "Thad's luffly, dey ought to baint a bicture of it." This was low comedy, but it was evident that money and power were falling into the hands of people in comparison with whom the leader of a village Soviet would be a gold-mine of judgment and culture. There were citizens travelling in luxury in 1928 and 1929 who, in the distortion of their new condition, had the human value of Pekinese, bivalves, cretins, goats. I remember the

Judge from some New York district who had taken his daughter to see the Bayeux Tapestries and made a scene in the papers advocating their segregation because one scene was immoral. But in those days life was like the race in *Alice in Wonderland,* there was a prize for every one.

The Jazz Age had had a wild youth and a heady middle age. There was the phase of the necking parties, the Leopold-Loeb murder (I remember the time my wife was arrested on Queensborough Bridge on the suspicion of being the "Bob-haired Bandit") and the John Held Clothes. In the second phase such phenomena as sex and murder became more mature, if much more conventional. Middle age must be served and pajamas came to the beach to save fat thighs and flabby calves from competition with the one-piece bathing-suit. Finally skirts came down and everything was concealed. Everybody was at scratch now. Let's go—

But it was not to be. Somebody had blundered and the most expensive orgy in history was over.

It ended two years ago,* because the utter confidence which was its essential prop received an enormous jolt, and it didn't take long for the flimsy structure to settle earthward. And after two years the Jazz Age seems as far away as the days before the War. It was borrowed time anyhow—the whole upper tenth of a nation living with the insouciance of grand ducs and the casualness of chorus girls. But moralizing is easy now and it was pleasant to be in one's twenties in such a certain and unworried time. Even when you were broke you didn't worry about money, because it was in such profusion around you. Toward the end one had a struggle to pay one's share; it was almost a favor to accept hospitality

* 1929

that required any travelling. Charm, notoriety, mere good manners, weighed more than money as a social asset. This was rather splendid, but things were getting thinner and thinner as the eternal necessary human values tried to spread over all that expansion. Writers were geniuses on the strength of one respectable book or play; just as during the War officers of four months' experience commanded hundreds of men, so there were now many little fish lording it over great big bowls. In the theatrical world extravagant productions were carried by a few second-rate stars, and so on up the scale into politics, where it was difficult to interest good men in positions of the highest importance and responsibility, importance and responsibility far exceeding that of business executives but which paid only five or six thousand a year.

Now once more the belt is tight and we summon the proper expression of horror as we look back at our wasted youth. Sometimes, though, there is a ghostly rumble among the drums, an asthmatic whisper in the trombones that swings me back into the early twenties when we drank wood alcohol and every day in every way grew better and better, and there was a first abortive shortening of the skirts, and girls all looked alike in sweater dresses, and people you didn't want to know said "Yes, we have no bananas," and it seemed only a question of a few years before the older people would step aside and let the world be run by those who saw things as they were—and it all seems rosy and romantic to us who were young then, because we will never feel quite so intensely about our surroundings any more.

My Lost City

MY LOST CITY

July, 1932

THERE was first the ferry boat moving softly from the Jersey shore at dawn—the moment crystalized into my first symbol of New York. Five years later when I was fifteen I went into the city from school to see Ina Claire in *The Quaker Girl* and Gertrude Bryan in *Little Boy Blue*. Confused by my hopeless and melancholy love for them both, I was unable to choose between them—so they blurred into one lovely entity, the girl. She was my second symbol of New York. The ferry boat stood for triumph, the girl for romance. In time I was to achieve some of both, but there was a third symbol that I have lost somewhere, and lost forever.

I found it on a dark April afternoon after five more years.

"Oh, Bunny," I yelled. *"Bunny!"*

He did not hear me—my taxi lost him, picked him up again half a block down the street. There were black spots of rain on the sidewalk and I saw him walking briskly through the crowd wearing a tan raincoat over his inevitable brown get-up; I noted with a shock that he was carrying a light cane.

"Bunny!" I called again, and stopped. I was still an undergraduate at Princeton while he had become a New Yorker. This was his afternoon walk, this hurry along with his stick through the gathering rain, and as I was not to meet him for an hour it seemed an intrusion to happen upon him engrossed in his private life. But the taxi kept pace with him and as I continued to watch I was impressed: he was no longer the shy little scholar of Holder Court—he walked with confidence, wrapped in his thoughts and looking straight ahead, and it was obvious that his new background was entirely sufficient to him. I knew that he had an apartment where he lived with three other men, released now from all undergraduate taboos, but there was something else that was nourishing him and I got my first impression of that new thing—the Metropolitan spirit.

Up to this time I had seen only the New York that offered itself for inspection—I was Dick Whittington up from the country gaping at the trained bears, or a youth of the Midi dazzled by the boulevards of Paris. I had come only to stare at the show, though the designers of the Woolworth Building and the Chariot Race Sign, the producers of musical comedies and problem plays, could ask for no more appreciative spectator, for I took the style and glitter of New York even above its own valuation. But I had never accepted any of the practically anonymous invitations to debutante balls that turned up in an undergraduate's mail, perhaps because I felt that no actuality could live up to my conception of New York's splendor. Moreover, she to whom I fatuously referred as "my girl" was a Middle Westerner, a fact which kept the warm center of the world out there, so I thought of

New York as essentially cynical and heartless—save for one night when she made luminous the Ritz Roof on a brief passage through.

Lately, however, I had definitely lost her and I wanted a man's world, and this sight of Bunny made me see New York as just that. A week before, Monsignor Fay had taken me to the Lafayette where there was spread before us a brilliant flag of food, called an *hors d'oeuvre*, and with it we drank claret that was as brave as Bunny's confident cane—but after all it was a restaurant and afterwards we would drive back over a bridge into the hinterland. The New York of undergraduate dissipation, of Bustanoby's, Shanley's, Jack's, had become a horror and though I returned to it, alas, through many an alcoholic mist, I felt each time a betrayal of a persistent idealism. My participance was prurient rather than licentious and scarcely one pleasant memory of it remains from those days; as Ernest Hemingway once remarked, the sole purpose of the cabaret is for unattached men to find complaisant women. All the rest is a wasting of time in bad air.

But that night, in Bunny's apartment, life was mellow and safe, a finer distillation of all that I had come to love at Princeton. The gentle playing of an oboe mingled with city noises from the street outside, which penetrated into the room with difficulty through great barricades of books; only the crisp tearing open of invitations by one man was a discordant note. I had found a third symbol of New York and I began wondering about the rent of such apartments and casting about for the appropriate friends to share one with me.

Fat chance—for the next two years I had as much control over my own destiny as a convict over the cut of his clothes. When I got back to New York in 1919 I was so entangled in life that a period of mellow monasticism in Washington Square was not to be dreamed of. The thing was to make enough money in the advertising business to rent a stuffy apartment for two in the Bronx. The girl concerned had never seen New York but she was wise enough to be rather reluctant. And in a haze of anxiety and unhappiness I passed the four most impressionable months of my life.

New York had all the iridescence of the beginning of the world. The returning troops marched up Fifth Avenue and girls were instinctively drawn East and North toward them —this was the greatest nation and there was gala in the air. As I hovered ghost-like in the Plaza Red Room of a Saturday afternoon, or went to lush and liquid garden parties in the East Sixties or tippled with Princetonians in the Biltmore Bar I was haunted always by my other life—my drab room in the Bronx, my square foot of the subway, my fixation upon the day's letter from Alabama—would it come and what would it say?—my shabby suits, my poverty, and love. While my friends were launching decently into life I had muscled my inadequate bark into midstream. The gilded youth circling around young Constance Bennett in the Club de Vingt, the classmates in the Yale-Princeton Club whooping up our first after-the-war reunion, the atmosphere of the millionaires' houses that I sometimes frequented—these things were empty for me, though I recognized them as impressive scenery and regretted that I was committed to other romance. The most hilarious luncheon table or the most moony cabaret—it was all the same; from them I returned eagerly to my home on Claremont Avenue—home because there might be a letter waiting outside the door. One by one my great dreams of New York became tainted. The remembered charm of Bunny's apartment faded with the rest when I interviewed a blowsy landlady in Greenwich Village. She told me I could bring girls to the room, and the idea filled me with dismay—why should I want to bring girls to my room?—I had a girl. I wandered through the town of 127th Street, resenting its vibrant life; or else I bought cheap theatre seats at Gray's drugstore and tried to lose myself for a few hours in my old passion for Broadway. I was a failure—mediocre at advertising work and unable to get started as a writer. Hating the city, I got roaring, weeping drunk on my last penny and went home. . . .

. . . Incalculable city. What ensued was only one of a thousand success stories of those gaudy days, but it plays a part in my own movie of New York. When I returned six months later the offices of editors and publishers were open to me, impresarios begged plays, the movies panted for screen material. To my bewilderment, I was adopted, not as a Middle Westerner, not even as a detached observer, but as the arch type of what New York wanted. This statement requires some account of the metropolis in 1920.

There was already the tall white city of today, already the feverish activity of the boom, but there was a general inarticulateness. As much as anyone the columnist F. P. A. guessed the pulse of the individual and the crowd, but shyly, as one watching from a window. Society and the native arts had not mingled—Ellen Mackay was not yet married to Irving Berlin. Many of Peter Arno's people would have been meaningless to the citizen of 1920, and save for F. P. A.'s column there was no forum for metropolitan urbanity.

Then, for just a moment, the "younger generation" idea became a fusion of many elements in New York life. People of fifty might pretend there was still a four hundred or Maxwell Bodenheim might pretend there was a Bohemia worth its paint and pencils—but the blending of the bright, gay, vigorous elements began then and for the first time there appeared a society a little livelier than the solid mahogany dinner parties of Emily Price Post. If this society produced the cocktail party, it also evolved Park Avenue wit and for the first time an educated European could envisage a trip to New York as something more amusing than a gold-trek into a formalized Australian Bush.

For just a moment, before it was demonstrated that I was unable to play the role, I, who knew less of New York than any reporter of six months standing and less of its society than any hall-room boy in a Ritz stag line, was pushed into the position not only of spokesman for the time but of the typical product of that same moment. I, or rather it was "we" now, did not know exactly what New York expected of us and found it rather confusing. Within a few months after our embarkation on the Metropolitan venture we scarcely knew any more who we were and we hadn't a notion what we were. A dive into a civic fountain, a casual brush with the law, was enough to get us into the gossip columns, and we were quoted on a variety of subjects we knew nothing about. Actually our "contacts" included half a dozen unmarried college friends and a few new literary acquaintances—I remember a lonesome Christmas when we had not one friend in the city, nor one house we could go to. Finding no nucleus to which we could cling, we became a small nucleus ourselves and gradually we fitted our disruptive personalities into the contemporary scene of New York. Or rather New York forgot us and let us stay.

This is not an account of the city's changes but of the changes in this writer's feeling for the city. From the confusion of the year 1920 I remember riding on top of a taxicab along deserted Fifth Avenue on a hot Sunday night, and a luncheon in the cool Japanese gardens at the Ritz with the wistful Kay Laurel and George Jean Nathan, and writing all night again and again, and paying too much for minute apartments, and buying magnificent but broken-down cars. The first speakeasies had arrived, the toddle was *passé*, the Montmartre was the smart place to dance and Lillian Tashman's fair hair weaved around the floor among the enliquored college boys. The plays were *Declassée* and *Sacred and Profane Love,* and at the Midnight Frolic you danced elbow to elbow with Marion Davies and perhaps picked out the vivacious Mary Hay in the pony chorus. We thought we were apart from all that; perhaps everyone thinks they are apart from their milieu. We felt like small children in a great bright unexplored barn. Summoned out to Griffith's studio on Long Island, we trembled in the presence of the familiar faces of the *Birth of a Nation;* later I realized that behind much of the entertainment that the city poured forth into the nation there were only a lot of rather lost and lonely people. The world of the picture actors was like our own in that it was in New York and not of it. It had little sense of itself and no center: when I first met Dorothy Gish I had the feeling that we were both standing on the North Pole and it was snowing. Since then they have found a home but it was not destined to be New York.

When bored we took our city with a Huysmans-like perversity. An afternoon alone in our "apartment" eating olive sandwiches and drinking a quart of Bushmill's whiskey presented by Zoë Atkins, then out into the freshly bewitched city, through strange doors into strange apartments with intermittent swings along in taxis through the soft nights. At last we were one with New York, pulling it after us through every portal. Even now I go into many flats with the sense that I have been there before or in the one above or below—was it the night I tried to disrobe in the *Scandals*, or the night when (as I read with astonishment in the paper next morning) "Fitzgerald Knocks Officer This Side of Paradise"? Successful scrapping not being among my accomplishments, I tried in vain to reconstruct the sequence of events which led up to this dénouement in Webster Hall. And lastly from that period I remember riding in a taxi one afternoon between very tall buildings under a mauve and rosy sky; I began to bawl because I had everything I wanted and knew I would never be so happy again.

It was typical of our precarious position in New York that when our child was to be born we played safe and went home to St. Paul—it seemed inappropriate to bring a baby into all that glamor and loneliness. But in a year we were back and we began doing the same things over again and not liking them so much. We had run through a lot, though we had retained an almost theatrical innocence by preferring the role of the observed to that of the observer. But innocence is no end in itself and as our minds unwillingly matured we began to see New York whole and try to save some of it for the selves we would inevitably become.

It was too late—or too soon. For us the city was inevitably linked up with Bacchic diversions, mild or fantastic. We could organize ourselves only on our return to Long Island and not always there. We had no incentive to meet the city half way. My first symbol was now a memory, for I knew that triumph is in oneself; my second one had grown commonplace—two of the actresses whom I had worshipped from afar in 1913 had dined in our house. But it filled me with a certain fear that even the third symbol had grown dim—the tranquillity of Bunny's apartment was not to be found in the ever-quickening city. Bunny himself was married, and about to become a father, other friends had gone to Europe, and the bachelors had become cadets of houses larger and more social than ours. By this time we "knew everybody"—which is to say most of those whom Ralph Barton would draw as in the orchestra on an opening night.

But we were no longer important. The flapper, upon whose activities the popularity of my first books was based, had become *passé* by 1923—anyhow in the East. I decided to crash Broadway with a play, but Broadway sent its scouts to Atlantic City and quashed the idea in advance, so I felt that, for the moment, the city and I had little to offer each other. I would take the Long Island atmosphere that I had familiarly breathed and materialize it beneath unfamiliar skies.

It was three years before we saw New York again. As the ship glided up the river, the city burst thunderously upon us in the early dusk—the white glacier of lower New York swooping down like a strand of a bridge to rise into uptown New York, a miracle of foamy light suspended by the stars. A band started to play on deck, but the majesty of the city made the march trivial and tinkling. From that moment I knew that New York, however often I might leave it, was home.

The tempo of the city had changed sharply. The uncertainties of 1920 were drowned in a steady golden roar and many of our friends had grown wealthy. But the restlessness of New York in 1927 approached hysteria. The parties were bigger—those of Condé Nast, for example, rivaled in their way the fabled balls of the nineties; the pace was faster—the catering to dissipation set an example to Paris;

the shows were broader, the buildings were higher, the morals were looser and the liquor was cheaper; but all these benefits did not really minister to much delight. Young people wore out early—they were hard and languid at twenty-one and save for Peter Arno none of them contributed anything new; perhaps Peter Arno and his collaborators said everything there was to say about the boom days in New York that couldn't be said by a jazz band. Many people who were not alcoholics were lit up four days out of seven, and frayed nerves were strewn everywhere; groups were held together by a generic nervousness and the hangover became a part of the day as well allowed-for as the Spanish siesta. Most of my friends drank too much—the more they were in tune to the times the more they drank. And as effort *per se* had no dignity against the mere bounty of those days in New York, a depreciatory word was found for it: a successful programme became a racket—I was in the literary racket.

We settled a few hours from New York and I found that every time I came to the city I was caught up into a complication of events that deposited me a few days later in a somewhat exhausted state on the train for Delaware. Whole sections of the city had grown rather poisonous, but invariably I found a moment of utter peace in riding south through Central Park at dark toward where the façade of 59th Street thrusts its lights through the trees. There again was my lost city, wrapped cool in its mystery and promise. But that detachment never lasted long—as the toiler must live in the city's belly, so I was compelled to live in its disordered mind.

Instead there were the speakeasies—the moving from

luxurious bars, which advertised in the campus publications of Yale and Princeton, to the beer gardens where the snarling face of the underworld peered through the German good nature of the entertainment, then on to strange and even more sinister localities where one was eyed by granite-faced boys and there was nothing left of joviality but only a brutishness that corrupted the new day into which one presently went out. Back in 1920 I shocked a rising young business man by suggesting a cocktail before lunch. In 1929 there was liquor in half the downtown offices, and a speakeasy in half the large buildings.

One was increasingly conscious of the speakeasy and of Park Avenue. In the past decade Greenwich Village, Washington Square, Murray Hill, the châteaux of Fifth Avenue had somehow disappeared, or become unexpressive of anything. The city was bloated, glutted, stupid with cake and circuses, and a new expression "Oh yeah?" summed up all the enthusiasm evoked by the announcement of the last super-skyscrapers. My barber retired on a half million bet in the market and I was conscious that the head waiters who bowed me, or failed to bow me, to my table were far, far wealthier than I. This was no fun—once again I had enough of New York and it was good to be safe on shipboard where the ceaseless revelry remained in the bar in transport to the fleecing rooms of France.

"What news from New York?"

"Stocks go up. A baby murdered a gangster."

"Nothing more?"

"Nothing. Radios blare in the street."

I once thought that there were no second acts in American lives, but there was certainly to be a second act to New

York's boom days. We were somewhere in North Africa when we heard a dull distant crash which echoed to the farthest wastes of the desert.

"What was that?"

"Did you hear it?"

"It was nothing."

"Do you think we ought to go home and see?"

"No—it was nothing."

In the dark autumn of two years later we saw New York again. We passed through curiously polite customs agents, and then with bowed head and hat in hand I walked reverently through the echoing tomb. Among the ruins a few childish wraiths still played to keep up the pretense that they were alive, betraying by their feverish voices and hectic cheeks the thinness of the masquerade. Cocktail parties, a last hollow survival from the days of carnival, echoed to the plaints of the wounded: "Shoot me, for the love of God, someone shoot me!", and the groans and wails of the dying: "Did you see that United States Steel is down three more points?" My barber was back at work in his shop; again the head waiters bowed people to their tables, if there were people to be bowed. From the ruins, lonely and inexplicable as the sphinx, rose the Empire State Building and, just as it had been a tradition of mine to climb to the Plaza Roof to take leave of the beautiful city, extending as far as eyes could reach, so now I went to the roof of the last and most magnificent of towers. Then I understood—everything was explained: I had discovered the crowning error of the city, its Pandora's box. Full of vaunting pride the New Yorker had climbed here and seen with dismay what he had never suspected, that the city was not the endless succession of canyons that he had supposed but that *it had limits*—from the tallest structure he saw for the first time that it faded out into the country on all sides, into an expanse of green and blue that alone was limitless. And with the awful realization that New York was a city after all and not a universe, the whole shining edifice that he had reared in his imagination came crashing to the ground. That was the rash gift of Alfred E. Smith to the citizens of New York.

Thus I take leave of my lost city. Seen from the ferry boat in the early morning, it no longer whispers of fantastic success and eternal youth. The whoopee mamas who prance before its empty parquets do not suggest to me the ineffable beauty of my dream girls of 1914. And Bunny, swinging along confidently with his cane toward his cloister in a carnival, has gone over to Communism and frets about the wrongs of southern mill workers and western farmers whose voices, fifteen years ago, would not have penetrated his study walls.

All is lost save memory, yet sometimes I imagine myself reading, with curious interest, a *Daily News* of the issue of 1945:

MAN OF FIFTY RUNS AMUCK IN NEW YORK
Fitzgerald Feathered Many Love Nests Cutie Avers Bumped Off By Outraged Gunman

So perhaps I am destined to return some day and find in the city new experiences that so far I have only read about. For the moment I can only cry out that I have lost my splendid mirage. Come back, come back, O glittering and white!

"SHOW MR. AND
MRS. F. TO
NUMBER—"

"Show Mr. and Mrs. F. to Number—"

By F. Scott and Zelda Fitzgerald

May-June, 1934

We are married. The Sibylline parrots are protesting the sway of the first bobbed heads in the Biltmore panelled luxe. The hotel is trying to look older.

The faded rose corridors of the Commodore end in subways and subterranean metropolises—a man sold us a broken Marmon and a wild burst of friends spent half an hour revolving in the revolving door.

There were lilacs open to the dawn near the boarding house in Westport where we sat up all night to finish a story. We quarreled in the gray morning dew about morals; and made up over a red bathing suit.

The Manhattan took us in one late night though we looked very young and gay. Ungratefully we packed the empty suitcase with spoons and the phone book and a big square pin-cushion.

The Traymore room was gray and the chaise longue big enough for a courtesan. The sound of the sea kept us awake.

Electric fans blew the smell of peaches and hot biscuit

and the cindery aroma of travelling salesmen through the New Willard halls in Washington.

But the Richmond hotel had a marble stair and long unopened rooms and marble statues of the gods lost somewhere in its echoing cells.

At the O. Henry in Greensville they thought a man and his wife ought not to be dressed alike in white knickerbockers in nineteen-twenty and we thought the water in the tubs ought not to run red mud.

Next day the summer whine of phonographs billowed out the skirts of the southern girls in Athens. There were so many smells in the drug stores and so much organdy and so many people just going somewhere. . . . We left at dawn.

1921

They were respectful in the Cecil in London; disciplined by the long majestuous twilights on the river and we were young but we were impressed anyway by the Hindus and the Royal Processions.

At the St. James and Albany in Paris we smelled up the room with an uncured Armenian goat-skin and put the unmelting "ice-cream" outside the window, and there were dirty postcards, but we were pregnant.

The Royal Danieli in Venice had a gambling machine and the wax of centuries over the window-sill and there were fine officers on the American destroyer. We had fun in a gondola feeling like a soft Italian song.

Bamboo curtains and an asthma patient complaining of the green plush and an ebony piano were all equally embalmed in the formal parlors of the Hôtel d'Italie in Florence.

But there were fleas on the gilded filigree of the Grand Hôtel in Rome; men from the British embassy scratched behind the palms; the clerks said it was the flea season.

Claridge's in London served strawberries in a gold dish, but the room was an inside room and gray all day, and the waiter didn't care whether we left or not, and he was our only contact.

In the fall we got to the Commodore in St. Paul, and while leaves blew up the streets we waited for our child to be born.

1922-1923

The Plaza was an etched hotel, dainty and subdued, with such a handsome head waiter that he never minded lending five dollars or borrowing a Rolls-Royce. We didn't travel much in those years.

1924

The Deux Mondes in Paris ended about a blue abysmal court outside our window. We bathed the daughter in the *bidet* by mistake and she drank the gin fizz thinking it was lemonade and ruined the luncheon table next day.

Goat was to eat in Grimm's Park Hotel in Hyères, and the bougainvillea was brittle as its own color in the hot white dust. Many soldiers loitered outside the gardens and brothels listening to the nickelodeons. The nights, smelling of honey-suckle and army leather, staggered up the mountain side and settled upon Mrs. Edith Wharton's garden.

At the Ruhl in Nice we decided on a room not facing the sea, on all the dark men being princes, on not being able to afford it even out of season. During dinner on the terrace, stars fell in our plates, and we tried to identify ourselves with the place by recognizing faces from the boat. But no-body passed and we were alone with the deep blue grandeur and the *filet de sole Ruhl* and the second bottle of champagne.

The Hôtel de Paris at Monte Carlo was like a palace in a detective story. Officials got us things: tickets and permis-sions, maps and newly portentous identities. We waited a good while in the formalized sun while they fitted us out with all we needed to be fitting guests of the Casino. Finally, taking control of the situation, we authoritatively sent the bell-boy for a tooth-brush.

Wistaria dripped in the court of the Hôtel d'Europe at Avignon and the dawn rumbled up in market carts. A lone lady in tweeds drank Martinis in the dingy bar. We met French friends at the Taverne Riche and listened to the bells of late afternoon reverberate along the city walls. The Palace of the Popes rose chimerically through the gold end of day over the broad still Rhône, while we did nothing, assiduously, under the plane trees on the opposite bank.

Like Henri IV, a French patriot fed his babies red wine in the Continental at St. Raphaël and there were no carpets because of summer, so echoes of the children's protestations fell pleasantly amidst the clatter of dishes and china. By this time we could identify a few words of French and felt ourselves part of the country.

The Hôtel du Cap at Antibes was almost deserted. The

heat of day lingered in the blue and white blocks of the balcony and from the great canvas mats our friends had spread along the terrace we warmed our sunburned backs and invented new cocktails.

The Miramare in Genoa festooned the dark curve of the shore with garlands of lights, and the shape of the hills was picked out of the darkness by the blaze from the windows of high hotels. We thought of the men parading the gay arcades as undiscovered Carusos but they all assured us that Genoa was a business city and very like America and Milan.

We got to Pisa in the dark and couldn't find the leaning tower until we passed it by accident leaving the Royal Victoria on our way out. It stood stark in a field by itself. The Arno was muddy and not half as insistent as it is in the cross-word puzzles.

Marion Crawford's mother died in the Quirinal Hotel at Rome. All the chamber-maids remember it and tell the visitors about how they spread the room with newspapers afterwards. The sitting-rooms are hermetically sealed and palms conceal the way to open the windows. Middle-aged English doze in the stale air and nibble stale-salted peanuts with the hotel's famous coffee, which comes out of a calliope-like device for filling it full of grounds, like the glass balls that make snow storms when shaken.

In the Hôtel des Princes at Rome we lived on Bel Paese cheese and Corvo wine and made friends with a delicate spinster who intended to stop there until she finished a three-volume history of the Borgias. The sheets were damp and the nights were perforated by the snores of the people next door, but we didn't mind because we could always come home down the stairs to the Via Sistina, and there were jonquils and beggars along that way. We were too superior

at that time to use the guide books and wanted to discover
the ruins for ourselves, which we did when we had exhausted the night-life and the market places and the cam-
pagna. We liked the Castello Sant'Angelo because of its round
mysterious unity and the river and the debris about its base.
It was exciting being lost between centuries in the Roman
dusk and taking your sense of direction from the Colosseum.

1925

At the hotel in Sorrento we saw the tarantella, but it was
a *real* one and we had seen so many more imaginative
adaptations. . . .

A southern sun drugged the court of the Quisisana to
somnolence. Strange birds protested their sleepiness beneath
the overwhelming cypress while Compton Mackenzie told
us why he lived in Capri: Englishmen must have an island.

The Tiberio was a high white hotel scalloped about the
base by the rounded roofs of Capri, cupped to catch rain
which never falls. We climbed to it through devious dark
alleys that house the island's Rembrandt butcher shops and
bakeries; then we climbed down again to the dark pagan
hysteria of Capri's Easter, the resurrection of the spirit of
the people.

When we got back to Marseilles, going north again, the
streets about the waterfront were bleached by the brightness
of the harbor and pedestrians gayly discussed errors of time
at little cafés on the corner. We were so damn glad of the
animation.

The hotel in Lyons wore an obsolete air and nobody ever

heard of Lyonnaise potatoes and we became so discouraged with touring that we left the little Renault there and took the train for Paris.

The Hôtel Florida had catacornered rooms; the gilt had peeled from the curtain fixtures.

When we started out again after a few months, touring south, we slept six in a room in Dijon (Hôtel du Dump, Pens. from 2 frs. Pouring water) because there wasn't any other place. Our friends considered themselves somewhat compromised but snored towards morning.

In Salies-de-Béarn in the Pyrenees we took a cure for colitis, disease of that year, and rested in a white pine room in the Hôtel Bellevue, flush with thin sun rolled down from the Pyrenees. There was a bronze statue of Henri IV on the mantel in our room, for his mother was born there. The boarded windows of the Casino were splotched with bird droppings—along the misty streets we bought canes with spears on the end and were a little discouraged about everything. We had a play on Broadway and the movies offered $60,000, but we were china people by then and it didn't seem to matter particularly.

When that was over, a hired limousine drove us to Toulouse, careening around the grey block of Carcassonne and through the long unpopulated planes of the Côte d'Argent. The Hôtel Tivollier, though ornate, had fallen into disuse. We kept ringing for the waiter to assure ourselves that life went on somewhere in the dingy crypt. He appeared resentfully and finally we induced him to give us so much beer that it heightened the gloom.

In the Hôtel O'Connor old ladies in white lace rocked their pasts to circumspection with the lullabyic motion of the hotel chairs. But they were serving blue twilights at the cafés along the Promenade des Anglais for the price of a porto, and we danced their tangos and watched girls shiver in the appropriate clothes for the Côte d'Azur. We went to the Perroquet with friends, one of us wearing a blue hyacinth and the other an ill temper which made him buy a wagon full of roasted chestnuts and immediately scatter their warm burnt odor like largesse over the cold spring night.

In the sad August of that year we made a trip to Mentone, ordering bouillabaisse in an aquarium-like pavillion by the sea across from the Hôtel Victoria. The hills were silver-olive, and of the true shape of frontiers.

Leaving the Riviera after a third summer, we called on a writer friend at the Hôtel Continental at Cannes. He was proud of his independence in adopting a black mongrel dog. He had a nice house and a nice wife and we envied his comfortable installations that gave the effect of his having retired from the world when he had really taken such of it as he wanted and confined it.

When we got back to America we went to the Roosevelt Hotel in Washington and to see one of our mothers. The cardboard hotels, bought in sets, made us feel as if we committed a desecration by living in them—we left the brick pavements and the elms and the heterogeneous qualities of Washington and went further south.

1927

It takes so long to get to California, and there were so many nickel handles, gadgets to avoid, buttons to invoke, and such a lot of newness and Fred Harvey, that when one of us thought he had appendicitis we got out at El Paso. A cluttered bridge dumps one in Mexico where the restaurants are trimmed with tissue paper and there are contraband perfumes—we admired the Texas rangers, not having seen men with guns on their hips since the war.

We reached California in time for an earthquake. It was sunny, and misty at night. White roses swung luminous in the mist from a trellis outside the Ambassador windows; a bright exaggerated parrot droned incomprehensible shouts in an aquamarine pool—of course everybody interpreted them to be obscenities; geraniums underscored the discipline of the California flora. We paid homage to the pale aloof concision of Diana Manners' primitive beauty and dined at Pickfair to marvel at Mary Pickford's dynamic subjugation of life. A thoughtful limousine carried us for California hours to be properly moved by the fragility of Lillian Gish, too aspiring for life, clinging vine-like to occultisms.

From there we went to the DuPont in Wilmington. A friend took us to tea in the mahogany recesses of an almost feudal estate, where the sun gleamed apologetically in the silver tea-service and there were four kinds of buns and four indistinguishable daughters in riding clothes and a mistress of the house too busily preserving the charm of another era to separate out the children. We leased a very big old mansion on the Delaware River. The squareness of the rooms and the sweep of the columns were to bring us a judicious tranquility. There were sombre horse-chestnuts in the yard and a white pine bending as graciously as a Japanese brush drawing.

We went up to Princeton. There was a new colonial inn, but the campus offered the same worn grassy parade ground for the romantic spectres of Light-Horse Harry Lee and

41

Aaron Burr. We loved the temperate shapes of Nassau Hall's old brick, and the way it seems still a tribunal of early American ideals, the elm walks and meadows, the college windows open to the spring—open, open to everything in life—for a minute.

The Negroes are in knee-breeches at the Cavalier in Virginia Beach. It is theatrically southern and its newness is a bit barren, but there is the best beach in America; at that time, before the cottages were built, there were dunes and the moon tripped, fell, in the sandy ripples along the seafront.

Next time we went, lost and driven now like the rest, it was a free trip north to Quebec. They thought maybe we'd write about it. The Château Frontenac was built of toy stone arches, a tin soldier's castle. Our voices were truncated by the heavy snow, the stalactite icicles on the low roofs turned the town to a wintry cave; we spent most of our time in an echoing room lined with skis, because the professional there gave us a good feeling about the sports at which we were so inept. He was later taken up by the DuPonts on the same basis and made a powder magnate or something.

When we decided to go back to France we spent the night at the Pennsylvania, manipulating the new radio earphones and the servidors, where a suit can be frozen to a cube by nightfall. We were still impressed by running ice-water, self-sustaining rooms that could function even if besieged with current events. We were so little in touch with the world that they gave us an impression of a crowded subway station.

The hotel in Paris was triangular-shaped and faced Saint-Germain-des-Prés. On Sundays we sat at the Deux Magots and watched the people, devout as an opera chorus, enter the old doors, or else watched the French read newspapers. There were long conversations about the ballet over sauerkraut in Lipps, and blank recuperative hours over books and prints in the dank Allée Bonaparte.

Now the trips away had begun to be less fun. The next one to Brittany broke at Le Mans. The lethargic town was crumbling away, pulverized by the heat of the white hot summer and only travelling salesmen slid their chairs preëmptorily about the uncarpeted dining room. Plane trees bordered the route to La Baule.

At the Palace in La Baule we felt raucous amidst so much chic restraint. Children bronzed on the bare blue-white beach while the tide went out so far as to leave them crabs and starfish to dig for in the sands.

1929

We went to America but didn't stay at hotels. When we got back to Europe we spent the first night at a sun-flushed hostelry, Bertolini's in Genoa. There was a green tile bath and a very attentive valet de chambre and there was ballet to practice, using the brass bedstead as a bar. It was good to see the brilliant flowers colliding in prismatic explosions over the terraced hillside and to feel ourselves foreigners again.

Reaching Nice, we went economically to the Beau Rivage, which offered many stained glass windows to the Mediterranean glare. It was spring and was brittly cold along the Promenade des Anglais, though the crowds moved persistently in a summer tempo. We admired the painted windows of the converted palaces on the Place Gambetta. Walking at dusk, the voices fell seductively through the nebulous twilight inviting us to share the first stars, but we were busy. We went to the cheap ballets of the Casino on the jettée and rode almost to Villefranche for *Salade Niçoise* and a very special bouillabaisse.

In Paris we economized again in a not-yet-dried cement hotel, the name of which we've forgotten. It cost us a good deal, for we ate out every night to avoid starchy table d'hôtes. Sylvia Beach invited us to dinner and the talk was all of the people who had discovered Joyce; we called on friends in better hotels: Zoë Akins, who had sought the picturesque of the open fires at Foyot's, and Esther at the Port-Royal, who took us to see Romaine Brooks' studio, a glass enclosed square of heaven swung high above Paris.

Then southward again, and wasting the dinner hour in an argument about which hotel: there was one in Beaune where Ernest Hemingway had liked the trout. Finally we decided to drive all night, and we ate well in a stable courtyard facing a canal—the green-white glare of Provence had already begun to dazzle us so that we didn't care whether the food was good or not. That night we stopped under the white-trunked trees to open the windshield to the moon and to the sweep of the south against our faces, and to better smell the fragrance rustling restlessly amidst the poplars.

At Fréjus Plage, they had built a new hotel, a barren structure facing the beach where the sailors bathe. We felt very superior remembering how we had been the first travellers to like the place in summer.

After the swimming at Cannes was over and the year's octopi had grown up in the crevices of the rocks, we started back to Paris. The night of the stock-market crash we stayed at the Beau Rivage in St. Raphaël in the room Ring Lardner had occupied another year. We got out as soon as we could because we had been there so many times before—it is sadder to find the past again and find it inadequate to the present than it is to have it elude you and remain forever a harmonious conception of memory.

At the Jules César in Arles we had a room that had once been a chapel. Following the festering waters of a stagnant canal we came to the ruins of a Roman dwelling-house. There was a blacksmith shop installed behind the proud columns and a few scattered cows ate the gold flowers off the meadow.

Then up and up; the twilit heavens expanded in the Cévennes valley, cracking the mountains apart, and there was a fearsome loneliness brooding on the flat tops. We crunched chestnut burrs on the road and aromatic smoke wound out of the mountain cottages. The Inn looked bad, the floors were covered with sawdust, but they gave us the best pheasant we ever ate and the best sausage, and the feather-beds were wonderful.

In Vichy, the leaves had covered the square about the wooden bandstand. Health advice was printed on the doors at the Hôtel du Parc and on the menu, but the salon was filled with people drinking champagne. We loved the massive trees in Vichy and the way the friendly town nestles in a hollow.

By the time we got to Tours, we had begun to feel like Cardinal Balue in his cage in the little Renault. The Hôtel de l'Univers was equally stuffy but after dinner we found a café crowded with people playing checkers and singing choruses and we felt we could go on to Paris after all.

Our cheap hotel in Paris had been turned into a girls'

school—we went to a nameless one in the Rue du Bac, where potted palms withered in the exhausted air. Through the thin partitions we witnessed the private lives and natural functions of our neighbors. We walked at night past the moulded columns of the Odéon and identified the gangrenous statue behind the Luxembourg fence as Catherine de Medici.

It was a trying winter and to forget bad times we went to Algiers. The Hôtel de l'Oasis was laced together by Moorish grills; and the bar was an outpost of civilization with people accentuating their eccentricities. Beggars in white sheets were propped against the walls, and the dash of colonial uniforms gave the cafés a desperate swashbuckling air. Berbers have plaintive trusting eyes but it is really Fate they trust.

In Bou Saada, the scent of amber was swept along the streets by wide desert cloaks. We watched the moon stumble over the sand hillocks in a dead white glow and believed the guide as he told us of a priest he knew who could wreck railroad trains by wishing. The Ouled Naïls were very brown and clean-cut girls, impersonal as they turned themselves into fitting instruments for sex by the ritual of their dance, jangling their gold to the tune of savage fidelities hid in the distant hills.

The world crumbled to pieces in Biskra; the streets crept through the town like streams of hot white lava. Arabs sold nougat and cakes of poisonous pink under the flare of open gas jets. Since *The Garden of Allah* and *The Sheik* the town has been filled with frustrate women. In the steep cobbled alleys we flinched at the brightness of mutton carcasses swung from the butchers' booths.

We stopped in El Kantara at a rambling inn whiskered

with wistaria. Purple dusk steamed up from the depths of a gorge and we walked to a painter's house, where, in the remoteness of those mountains, he worked at imitations of Meissonier.

Then Switzerland and another life. Spring bloomed in the gardens of the Grand Hôtel in Glion, and a panorama world scintillated in the mountain air. The sun steamed delicate blossoms loose from the rocks while far below glinted the lake of Geneva.

Beyond the balustrade of the Lausanne Palace, sailboats plume themselves in the breeze like birds. Willow trees weave lacy patterns on the gravel terrace. The people are chic fugitives from life and death, rattling their teacups in querulous emotion on the deep protective balcony. They spell the names of hotels and cities with flowerbeds and laburnum in Switzerland and even the street lights wore crowns of verbena.

1931

Leisurely men played checkers in the restaurant of the Hôtel de la Paix in Lausanne. The depression had become frank in the American papers so we wanted to get back home.

But we went to Annecy for two weeks in summer, and said at the end that we'd never go there again because those weeks had been perfect and no other time could match them. First we lived at the Beau-Rivage, a rambler rose-covered hotel, with a diving platform wedged beneath our window between the sky and the lake, but there were enormous flies on the raft so we moved across the lake to Menthon. The water was greener there and the shadows long and cool and the scraggly gardens staggered up the shelved precipice to the Hôtel Palace. We played tennis on the baked clay courts and fished tentatively from a low brick wall. The heat of summer seethed in the resin of the white pine bath-houses. We walked at night towards a café blooming with Japanese lanterns, white shoes gleaming like radium in the damp darkness. It was like the good gone times when we still believed in summer hotels and the philosophies of popular songs. Another night we danced a Wiener waltz, and just simply swep' around.

At the Caux Palace, a thousand yards in the air, we tea-danced on the uneven boards of a pavilion and sopped our toast in mountain honey.

When we passed through Munich the Regina-Palast was empty; they gave us a suite where the princes stayed in the days when royalty travelled. The young Germans stalking the ill-lit streets wore a sinister air—the talk that underscored the beer-garden waltzes was of war and hard times. Thornton Wilder took us to a famous restaurant where the beer deserved the silver mugs it was served in. We went to see the chérished witnesses to a lost cause; our voices echoed through the planetarium and we lost our orientation in the deep blue cosmic presentation of how things are.

In Vienna, the Bristol was the best hotel and they were glad to have us because it, too, was empty. Our windows looked out on the mouldy baroque of the Opera over the tops of sorrowing elms. We dined at the widow Sacher's— over the oak panelling hung a print of Franz Joseph going some happier place many years ago in a coach; one of the Rothschilds dined behind a leather screen. The city was poor already, or still, and the faces about us were harassed and defensive.

We stayed a few days at the Vevey Palace on Lake Geneva. The trees in the hotel gardens were the tallest we had ever seen and gigantic lonely birds fluttered over the surface of the lake. Farther along there was a gay little beach with a modern bar where we sat on the sands and discussed stomachs.

We motored back to Paris: that is, we sat nervously in our six horse-power Renault. At the famous Hôtel de la Cloche in Dijon we had a nice room with a very complicated mechanical inferno of a bath, which the valet proudly referred to as American plumbing.

In Paris for the last time, we installed ourselves amidst the faded grandeurs of the Hôtel Majestic. We went to the Exposition and yielded up our imaginations to gold-lit facsimiles of Bali. Lonely flooded rice fields of lonely far-off islands told us an immutable story of work and death. The juxtaposition of so many replicas of so many civilizations was confusing, and depressing.

Back in America we stayed at the New Yorker because the advertisements said it was cheap. Everywhere quietude was sacrificed to haste and, momentarily, it seemed an impossible world, even though lustrous from the roof in the blue dusk.

In Alabama, the streets were sleepy and remote and a calliope on parade gasped out the tunes of our youth. There was sickness in the family and the house was full of nurses so we stayed at the big new elaborate Jefferson Davis. The old houses near the business section were falling to pieces at last. New bungalows lined the cedar drives on the outskirts; four-o'clocks bloomed beneath the old iron deer and arbor-

vitae boxed the prim brick walks while vigorous weeds up-
rooted the pavements. Nothing had happened there since
the Civil War. Everybody had forgotten why the hotel had
been erected, and the clerk gave us three rooms and four
baths for nine dollars a day. We used one as a sitting-room
so the bell-boys would have some place to sleep when we
rang for them.

1932

At the biggest hotel in Biloxi we read *Genesis* and watched
the sea pave the deserted shore with a mosaic of black twigs.

We went to Florida. The bleak marshes were punctuated
by biblical admonitions to a better life; abandoned fishing
boats disintegrated in the sun. The Don Ce-sar Hotel in
Pass-A-Grille stretched lazily over the stubbed wilderness,
surrendering its shape to the blinding brightness of the gulf.
Opalescent shells cupped the twilight on the beach and a
stray dog's footprints in the wet sand staked out his claim to
a free path round the ocean. We walked at night and discussed the Pythagorean theory of numbers, and we fished
by day. We were sorry for the deep-sea bass and the amber-
jacks—they seemed such easy game and no sport at all.
Reading the *Seven Against Thebes,* we browned on a lonely
beach. The hotel was almost empty and there were so many
waiters waiting to be off that we could hardly eat our meals.

The room in the Algonquin was high up amidst the gilded domes of New York. Bells chimed hours that had yet to penetrate the shadowy streets of the canyon. It was too hot in the room, but the carpets were soft and the room was isolated by dark corridors outside the door and bright façades outside the window. We spent much time getting ready for theatres. We saw Georgia O'Keefe's pictures and it was a deep emotional experience to abandon oneself to that majestic aspiration so adequately fitted into eloquent abstract forms.

For years we had wanted to go to Bermuda. We went. The Elbow Beach Hotel was full of honeymooners, who scintillated so persistently in each other's eyes that we cynically moved. The Hotel St. George was nice. Bougain-villea cascaded down the tree trunks and long stairs passed by deep mysteries taking place behind native windows. Cats slept along the balustrade and lovely children grew. We rode bicycles along the wind-swept causeways and stared in a dreamy daze at such phenomena as roosters scratching amidst the sweet alyssum. We drank sherry on a veranda above the bony backs of horses tethered in the public square. We had travelled a lot, we thought. Maybe this would be the last trip for a long while. We thought Bermuda was a nice place to be the last one of so many years of travelling.

THE CRACK-UP

THE CRACK-UP

February, 1936

O<small>F</small> course all life is a process of breaking down, but the blows that do the dramatic side of the work—the big sudden blows that come, or seem to come, from outside—the ones you remember and blame things on and, in moments of weakness, tell your friends about, don't show their effect all at once. There is another sort of blow that comes from within—that you don't feel until it's too late to do anything about it, until you realize with finality that in some regard you will never be as good a man again. The first sort of breakage seems to happen quick—the second kind happens almost without your knowing it but is realized suddenly indeed.

Before I go on with this short history, let me make a general observation—the test of a first-rate intelligence is the ability to hold two opposed ideas in the mind at the same time, and still retain the ability to function. One should, for example, be able to see that things are hopeless and yet be determined to make them otherwise. This philosophy fitted

55

on to my early adult life, when I saw the improbable, the implausible, often the "impossible," come true. Life was something you dominated if you were any good. Life yielded easily to intelligence and effort, or to what proportion could be mustered of both. It seemed a romantic business to be a successful literary man—you were not ever going to be as famous as a movie star but what note you had was probably longer-lived—you were never going to have the power of a man of strong political or religious convictions but you were certainly more independent. Of course within the practice of your trade you were forever unsatisfied—but I, for one, would not have chosen any other.

As the twenties passed, with my own twenties marching a little ahead of them, my two juvenile regrets—at not being big enough (or good enough) to play football in college, and at not getting overseas during the war—resolved themselves into childish waking dreams of imaginary heroism that were good enough to go to sleep on in restless nights. The big problems of life seemed to solve themselves, and if the business of fixing them was difficult, it made one too tired to think of more general problems.

Life, ten years ago, was largely a personal matter. I must hold in balance the sense of the futility of effort and the sense of the necessity to struggle; the conviction of the inevitability of failure and still the determination to "succeed"—and, more than these, the contradiction between the dead hand of the past and the high intentions of the future. If I could do this through the common ills—domestic, professional and personal—then the ego would continue as an arrow shot from nothingness to nothingness with such force that only gravity would bring it to earth at last.

For seventeen years, with a year of deliberate loafing and

resting out in the center—things went on like that, with a
new chore only a nice prospect for the next day. I was living
hard, too, but: "Up to forty-nine it'll be all right," I said. "I
can count on that. For a man who's lived as I have, that's
all you could ask."

—And then, ten years this side of forty-nine, I suddenly
realized that I had prematurely cracked.

II

Now a man can crack in many ways—can crack in the
head—in which case the power of decision is taken from you
by others! or in the body, when one can but submit to the
white hospital world; or in the nerves. William Seabrook
in an unsympathetic book tells, with some pride and a movie
ending, of how he became a public charge. What led to his
alcoholism or was bound up with it, was a collapse of his
nervous system. Though the present writer was not so entangled—having at the time not tasted so much as a glass of
beer for six months—it was his nervous reflexes that were
giving way—too much anger and too many tears.

Moreover, to go back to my thesis that life has a varying
offensive, the realization of having cracked was not simul-
taneous with a blow, but with a reprieve.

Not long before, I had sat in the office of a great doctor
and listened to a grave sentence. With what, in retrospect,
seems some equanimity, I had gone on about my affairs in
the city where I was then living, not caring much, not thinking how much had been left undone, or what would become
of this and that responsibility, like people do in books; I was
well insured and anyhow I had been only a mediocre care-

57

taker of most of the things left in my hands, even of my talent.

But I had a strong sudden instinct that I must be alone. I didn't want to see any people at all. I had seen so many people all my life—I was an average mixer, but more than average in a tendency to identify myself, my ideas, my destiny, with those of all classes that I came in contact with. I was always saving or being saved—in a single morning I would go through the emotions ascribable to Wellington at Waterloo. I lived in a world of inscrutable hostiles and inalienable friends and supporters.

But now I wanted to be absolutely alone and so arranged a certain insulation from ordinary cares.

It was not an unhappy time. I went away and there were fewer people. I found I was good-and-tired. I could lie around and was glad to, sleeping or dozing sometimes twenty hours a day and in the intervals trying resolutely not to think—instead I made lists—made lists and tore them up, hundreds of lists: of cavalry leaders and football players and cities, and popular tunes and pitchers, and happy times, and hobbies and houses lived in and how many suits since I left the army and how many pairs of shoes (I didn't count the suit I bought in Sorrento that shrunk, nor the pumps and dress shirt and collar that I carried around for years and never wore, because the pumps got damp and grainy and the shirt and collar got yellow and starch-rotted). And lists of women I'd liked, and of the times I had let myself be snubbed by people who had not been my betters in character or ability.

—And then suddenly, surprisingly, I got better.

—And cracked like an old plate as soon as I heard the news.

That is the real end of this story. What was to be done about it will have to rest in what used to be called the "womb of time." Suffice it to say that after about an hour of solitary pillow-hugging, I began to realize that for two years my life had been a drawing on resources that I did not possess, that I had been mortgaging myself physically and spiritually up to the hilt. What was the small gift of life given back in comparison to that?—when there had once been a pride of direction and a confidence in enduring independence.

I realized that in those two years, in order to preserve something—an inner hush maybe, maybe not—I had weaned myself from all the things I used to love—that every act of life from the morning tooth-brush to the friend at dinner had become an effort. I saw that for a long time I had not liked people and things, but only followed the rickety old pretense of liking. I saw that even my love for those closest to me was become only an attempt to love, that my casual relations—with an editor, a tobacco seller, the child of a friend, were only what I remembered I *should* do, from other days. All in the same month I became bitter about such things as the sound of the radio, the advertisements in the magazines, the screech of tracks, the dead silence of the country—contemptuous at human softness, immediately (if secretively) quarrelsome toward hardness —hating the night when I couldn't sleep and hating the day because it went toward night. I slept on the heart side now because I knew that the sooner I could tire that out, even a little, the sooner would come that blessed hour of nightmare which, like a catharsis, would enable me to better meet the new day.

There were certain spots, certain faces I could look at. Like most Middle Westerners, I have never had any but the

59

vaguest race prejudices—I always had a secret yen for the lovely Scandinavian blondes who sat on porches in St. Paul but hadn't emerged enough economically to be part of what was then society. They were too nice to be "chickens" and too quickly off the farmlands to seize a place in the sun, but I remember going round blocks to catch a single glimpse of shining hair—the bright shock of a girl I'd never know. This is urban, unpopular talk. It strays afield from the fact that in these latter days I couldn't stand the sight of Celts, English, Politicians, Strangers, Virginians, Negroes (light or dark), Hunting People, or retail clerks, and middlemen in general, all writers (I avoided writers very carefully because they can perpetuate trouble as no one else can)—and all the classes as classes and most of them as members of their class . . .

Trying to cling to something, I liked doctors and girl children up to the age of about thirteen and well-brought-up boy children from about eight years old on. I could have peace and happiness with these few categories of people. I forgot to add that I liked old men—men over seventy, sometimes over sixty if their faces looked seasoned. I liked Katharine Hepburn's face on the screen, no matter what was said about her pretentiousness, and Miriam Hopkins' face, and old friends if I only saw them once a year and could remember their ghosts.

All rather inhuman and undernourished, isn't it? Well, that, children, is the true sign of cracking up.

It is not a pretty picture. Inevitably it was carted here and there within its frame and exposed to various critics. One of them can only be described as a person whose life makes other people's lives seem like death—even this time when she was cast in the usually unappealing role of Job's

comforter. In spite of the fact that this story is over, let me
append our conversation as a sort of postscript:

"Instead of being so sorry for yourself, listen—" she said.
(She always says "Listen," because she thinks while she
talks—*really* thinks.) So she said: "Listen. Suppose this
wasn't a crack in you—suppose it was a crack in the Grand
Canyon."

"The crack's in me," I said heroically.

"Listen! The world only exists in your eyes—your conception of it. You can make it as big or as small as you want
to. And you're trying to be a little puny individual. By God,
if I ever cracked, I'd try to make the world crack with me.
Listen! The world only exists through your apprehension
of it, and so it's much better to say that it's not you that's
cracked—it's the Grand Canyon."

"Baby et up all her Spinoza?"

"I don't know anything about Spinoza. I know—" She
spoke, then, of old woes of her own, that seemed, in the
telling, to have been more dolorous than mine, and how she
had met them, over-ridden them, beaten them.

I felt a certain reaction to what she said, but I am a slow-
thinking man, and it occurred to me simultaneously that
of all natural forces, vitality is the incommunicable one. In
days when juice came into one as an article without duty,
one tried to distribute it—but always without success; to
further mix metaphors, vitality never "takes." You have it
or you haven't it, like health or brown eyes or honor or a
baritone voice. I might have asked some of it from her,
neatly wrapped and ready for home cooking and digestion,
but I could never have got it—not if I'd waited around for
a thousand hours with the tin cup of self-pity. I could walk
from her door, holding myself very carefully like cracked

crockery, and go away into the world of bitterness, where I was making a home with such materials as are found there—and quote to myself after I left her door:

"Ye are the salt of the earth. But if the salt hath lost its savour, wherewith shall it be salted?"

Matthew 5-13.

PASTING IT TOGETHER

March, 1936

In a previous article this writer told about his realization that what he had before him was not the dish that he had ordered for his forties. In fact—since he and the dish were one, he described himself as a cracked plate, the kind that one wonders whether it is worth preserving. Your editor thought that the article suggested too many aspects without regarding them closely, and probably many readers felt the same way—and there are always those to whom all self-revelation is contemptible, unless it ends with a noble thanks to the gods for the Unconquerable Soul.

But I had been thanking the gods too long, and thanking them for nothing. I wanted to put a lament into my record, without even the background of the Euganean Hills to give it color. There weren't any Euganean hills that I could see.

Sometimes, though, the cracked plate has to be retained in the pantry, has to be kept in service as a household necessity. It can never again be warmed on the stove nor shuffled with the other plates in the dishpan; it will not be brought out for company, but it will do to hold crackers late at night or to go into the ice box under left-overs . . .

Hence this sequel—a cracked plate's further history.

Now the standard cure for one who is sunk is to consider those in actual destitution or physical suffering—this is an all-weather beatitude for gloom in general and fairly salutory day-time advice for everyone. But at three o'clock in the morning, a forgotten package has the same tragic importance as a death sentence, and the cure doesn't work—and in a real dark night of the soul it is always three o'clock in the morning, day after day. At that hour the tendency is to refuse to face things as long as possible by retiring into an infantile dream—but one is continually startled out of this by various contacts with the world. One meets these occasions as quickly and carelessly as possible and retires once more back into the dream, hoping that things will adjust themselves by some great material or spiritual bonanza. But as the withdrawal persists there is less and less chance of the bonanza—one is not waiting for the fade-out of a single sorrow, but rather being an unwilling witness of an execution, the disintegration of one's own personality . . .

Unless madness or drugs or drink come into it, this phase comes to a dead-end, eventually, and is succeeded by a vacuous quiet. In this you can try to estimate what has been sheared away and what is left. Only when this quiet came to me, did I realize that I had gone through two parallel experiences.

The first time was twenty years ago, when I left Princeton in junior year with a complaint diagnosed as malaria. It transpired, through an X-ray taken a dozen years later, that it had been tuberculosis—a mild case, and after a few months of rest I went back to college. But I had lost certain offices, the chief one was the presidency of the Triangle Club, a musical comedy idea, and also I dropped back a class. To me college would never be the same. There were to be no badges of pride, no medals, after all. It seemed on one March afternoon that I had lost every single thing I wanted—and that night was the first time that I hunted down the spectre of womanhood that, for a little while, makes everything else seem unimportant.

Years later I realized that my failure as a big shot in college was all right—instead of serving on committees, I took a beating on English poetry; when I got the idea of what it was all about, I set about learning how to write. On Shaw's principle that "If you don't get what you like, you better like what you get," it was a lucky break—at the moment it was a harsh and bitter business to know that my career as a leader of men was over.

Since that day I have not been able to fire a bad servant, and I am astonished and impressed by people who can. Some old desire for personal dominance was broken and gone. Life around me was a solemn dream, and I lived on the letters I wrote to a girl in another city. A man does not recover from such jolts—he becomes a different person and, eventually, the new person finds new things to care about.

The other episode parallel to my current situation took place after the war, when I had again over-extended my flank. It was one of those tragic loves doomed for lack of money, and one day the girl closed it out on the basis of common sense. During a long summer of despair I wrote a novel instead of letters, so it came out all right, but it came out all right for a different person. The man with the jingle of money in his pocket who married the girl a year later would always cherish an abiding distrust, an animosity, toward the leisure class—not the conviction of a revolutionist but the smouldering hatred of a peasant. In the years since then I have never been able to stop wondering where my friends' money came from, nor to stop thinking that at one time a sort of *droit de seigneur* might have been exercised to give one of them my girl.

For sixteen years I lived pretty much as this latter person, distrusting the rich, yet working for money with which to share their mobility and the grace that some of them brought into their lives. During this time I had plenty of the usual horses shot from under me—I remember some of their names—*Punctured Pride, Thwarted Expectation, Faithless, Show-off, Hard Hit, Never Again*. And after awhile I wasn't twenty-five, then not even thirty-five, and nothing was quite as good. But in all these years I don't remember a moment of discouragement. I saw honest men through moods of suicidal gloom—some of them gave up and died; others adjusted themselves and went on to a larger success than mine; but my morale never sank below the level of self-disgust when I had put on some unsightly personal show. Trouble has no necessary connection with discouragement—discouragement has a germ of its own, as different from trouble as arthritis is different from a stiff joint.

When a new sky cut off the sun last spring, I didn't at first relate it to what had happened fifteen or twenty years ago. Only gradually did a certain family resemblance come through—an over-extension of the flank, a burning of the candle at both ends; a call upon physical resources that I did not command, like a man over-drawing at his bank. In its impact this blow was more violent than the other two but it was the same in kind—a feeling that I was standing at twilight on a deserted range, with an empty rifle in my hands and the targets down. No problem set—simply a silence with only the sound of my own breathing.

In this silence there was a vast irresponsibility toward every obligation, a deflation of all my values. A passionate belief in order, a disregard of motives or consequences in favor of guess work and prophecy, a feeling that craft and industry would have a place in any world—one by one, these and other convictions were swept away. I saw that the novel, which at my maturity was the strongest and supplest medium for conveying thought and emotion from one human being to another, was becoming subordinated to a mechanical and communal art that, whether in the hands of Hollywood merchants or Russian idealists, was capable of reflecting only the tritest thought, the most obvious emotion. It was an art in which words were subordinate to images, where personality was worn down to the inevitable low gear of collaboration. As long past as 1930, I had a hunch that the talkies would make even the best selling novelist as archaic as silent pictures. People still read, if only Professor Canby's book of the month—curious children nosed at the slime of Mr. Tiffany Thayer in the drugstore libraries—but there was a rankling indignity, that to me had become almost an obsession, in seeing the power of the written word subordinated to another power, a more glittering, a grosser power . . .

I set that down as an example of what haunted me during the long night—this was something I could neither accept nor struggle against, something which tended to make my efforts obsolescent, as the chain stores have crippled the small merchant, an exterior force, unbeatable—

(I have the sense of lecturing now, looking at a watch on the desk before me and seeing how many more minutes—).

Well, when I had reached this period of silence, I was forced into a measure that no one ever adopts voluntarily:

66

I was impelled to think. God, was it difficult! The moving about of great secret trunks. In the first exhausted halt, I wondered whether I had ever thought. After a long time I came to these conclusions, just as I write them here:

(1) That I had done very little thinking, save within the problems of my craft. For twenty years a certain man had been my intellectual conscience. That was Edmund Wilson.

(2) That another man represented my sense of the "good life," though I saw him once in a decade, and since then he might have been hung. He is in the fur business in the Northwest and wouldn't like his name set down here. But in difficult situations I had tried to think what *he* would have thought, how *he* would have acted.

(3) That a third contemporary had been an artistic conscience to me—I had not imitated his infectious style, because my own style, such as it is, was formed before he published anything, but there was an awful pull toward him when I was on a spot.

(4) That a fourth man had come to dictate my relations with other people when these relations were successful: how to do, what to say. How to make people at least momentarily happy (in opposition to Mrs. Post's theories of how to make everyone thoroughly uncomfortable with a sort of systematized vulgarity). This always confused me and made me want to go out and get drunk, but this man had seen the game, analyzed it and beaten it, and his word was good enough for me.

(5) That my political conscience had scarcely existed for ten years save as an element of irony in my stuff. When I became again concerned with the system I should function under, it was a man much younger than myself who brought it to me, with a mixture of passion and fresh air.

So there was not an "I" any more—not a basis on which I could organize my self-respect—save my limitless capacity for toil that it seemed I possessed no more. It was strange to have no self—to be like a little boy left alone in a big house, who knew that now he could do anything he wanted to do, but found that there was nothing that he wanted to do—

(The watch is past the hour and I have barely reached my thesis. I have some doubts as to whether this is of general interest, but if anyone wants more, there is plenty left, and your editor will tell me. If you've had enough, say so—but not too loud, because I have the feeling that someone, I'm not sure who, is sound asleep—someone who could have helped me to keep my shop open. It wasn't Lenin, and it wasn't God.)

HANDLE WITH CARE

April, 1936

I have spoken in these pages of how an exceptionally optimistic young man experienced a crack-up of all values, a crack-up that he scarcely knew of until long after it occurred. I told of the succeeding period of desolation and of the necessity of going on, but without benefit of Henley's familiar heroics, "my head is bloody but unbowed." For a check-up of my spiritual liabilities indicated that I had no particular head to be bowed or unbowed. Once I had had a heart but that was about all I was sure of.

This was at least a starting place out of the morass in which I floundered: "I felt—therefore I was." At one time or another there had been many people who had leaned on me, come to me in difficulties or written me from afar, believed implicitly in my advice and my attitude toward life. The dullest platitude monger or the most unscrupulous Rasputin who can influence the destinies of many people must have some individuality, so the question became one of finding why and where I had changed, where was the leak through which, unknown to myself, my enthusiasm and my vitality had been steadily and prematurely trickling away.

One harassed and despairing night I packed a brief case and went off a thousand miles to think it over. I took a dollar room in a drab little town where I knew no one and sunk all the money I had with me in a stock of potted meat, crackers and apples. But don't let me suggest that the change from a rather overstuffed world to a comparative asceticism was any Research Magnificent—I only wanted absolute quiet to think out why I had developed a sad attitude toward sadness, a melancholy attitude toward melancholy and a tragic attitude toward tragedy—*why I had become identified with the objects of my horror or compassion.*

Does this seem a fine distinction? It isn't: identification such as this spells the death of accomplishment. It is something like this that keeps insane people from working. Lenin did not willingly endure the sufferings of his proletariat, nor Washington of his troops, nor Dickens of his London poor. And when Tolstoy tried some such merging of himself with the objects of his attention, it was a fake and a failure. I mention these because they are the men best known to us all.

It was dangerous mist. When Wordsworth decided that "there had passed away a glory from the earth," he felt no compulsion to pass away with it, and the Fiery Particle Keats never ceased his struggle against t. b. nor in his last moments relinquished his hope of being among the English poets.

My self-immolation was something sodden-dark. It was very distinctly not modern—yet I saw it in others, saw it in a dozen men of honor and industry since the war. (I heard you, but that's too easy—there were Marxians among these men.) I had stood by while one famous contemporary of mine played with the idea of the Big Out for half a year; I had watched when another, equally eminent, spent months in an asylum unable to endure any contact with his fellow men. And of those who had given up and passed on I could list a score.

This led me to the idea that the ones who had survived had made some sort of clean break. This is a big word and is no parallel to a jail-break when one is probably headed for a new jail or will be forced back to the old one. The famous "Escape" or "run away from it all" is an excursion in a trap even if the trap includes the south seas, which are only for those who want to paint them or sail them. A clean break is something you cannot come back from; that is irretrievable because it makes the past cease to exist. So, since I could no longer fulfill the obligations that life had set for me or that I had set for myself, why not slay the empty shell who had been posturing at it for four years? I must continue to be a writer because that was my only way of life, but I would cease any attempts to be a person—to be kind, just or generous. There were plenty of counterfeit coins around that would pass instead of these and I knew where I could get them at a nickel on the dollar. In thirty-nine years an observant eye has learned to detect where the milk is watered and the sugar is sanded, the rhinestone passed for diamond and the stucco for stone. There was to be no more giving of myself—all giving was to be outlawed henceforth under a new name, and that name was Waste.

The decision made me rather exuberant, like anything that is both real and new. As a sort of beginning there was a whole shaft of letters to be tipped into the waste basket when I went home, letters that wanted something for nothing—to read this man's manuscript, market this man's poem, speak free on the radio, indite notes of introduction, give this interview, help with the plot of this play, with this domestic situation, perform this act of thoughtfulness or charity.

The conjuror's hat was empty. To draw things out of it had long been a sort of sleight of hand, and now, to change the metaphor, I was off the dispensing end of the relief roll forever.

The heady villainous feeling continued.

I felt like the beady-eyed men I used to see on the commuting train from Great Neck fifteen years back—men who didn't care whether the world tumbled into chaos tomorrow if it spared their houses. I was one with them now, one with the smooth articles who said:

"I'm sorry but business is business." Or:

"You ought to have thought of that before you got into this trouble." Or:

"I'm not the person to see about that."

And a smile—ah, I would get me a smile. I'm still working on that smile. It is to combine the best qualities of a hotel manager, an experienced old social weasel, a headmaster on visitors' day, a colored elevator man, a pansy pulling a profile, a producer getting stuff at half its market value, a trained nurse coming on a new job, a body-vender in her first rotogravure, a hopeful extra swept near the camera, a ballet dancer with an infected toe, and of course the great beam of loving kindness common to all those from Washington to Beverly Hills who must exist by virtue of the contorted pan.

The voice too—I am working with a teacher on the voice. When I have perfected it the larynx will show no ring of conviction except the conviction of the person I am talking to. Since it will be largely called upon for the elicitation of the word "Yes," my teacher (a lawyer) and I are concentrating on that, but in extra hours. I am learning to bring into it that polite acerbity that makes people feel that far from being welcome they are not even tolerated and are under continual and scathing analysis at every moment. These times will of course not coincide with the smile. This will be reserved exclusively for those from whom I have nothing to gain, old worn-out people or young struggling people. They won't mind—what the hell, they get it most of the time anyhow.

But enough. It is not a matter of levity. If you are young and you should write asking to see me and learn how to be a sombre literary man writing pieces upon the state of emotional exhaustion that often overtakes writers in their prime —if you should be so young and so fatuous as to do this, I would not do so much as acknowledge your letter, unless you were related to someone very rich and important indeed. And if you were dying of starvation outside my window, I would go out quickly and give you the smile and the voice (if no longer the hand) and stick around till somebody raised a nickel to phone for the ambulance, that is if I thought there would be any copy in it for me.

I have now at last become a writer only. The man I had persistently tried to be became such a burden that I have "cut him loose" with as little compunction as a Negro lady cuts loose a rival on Saturday night. Let the good people function as such—let the overworked doctors die in harness, with one week's "vacation" a year that they can devote to straightening out their family affairs, and let the under-worked doctors scramble for cases at one dollar a throw; let the soldiers be killed and enter immediately into the Val-halla of their profession. That is their contract with the gods. A writer need have no such ideals unless he makes them for himself, and this one has quit. The old dream of being an entire man in the Goethe-Byron-Shaw tradition, with an opulent American touch, a sort of combination of J. P. Morgan, Topham Beauclerk and St. Francis of Assisi, has been relegated to the junk heap of the shoulder pads worn for one day on the Princeton freshman football field and the overseas cap never worn overseas.

So what? This is what I think now: that the natural state of the sentient adult is a qualified unhappiness. I think also that in an adult the desire to be finer in grain than you are, "a constant striving" (as those people say who gain their bread by saying it) only adds to this unhappiness in the end —that end that comes to our youth and hope. My own happiness in the past often approached such an ecstasy that I could not share it even with the person dearest to me but had to walk it away in quiet streets and lanes with only fragments of it to distil into little lines in books—and I think that my happiness, or talent for self-delusion or what you will, was an exception. It was not the natural thing but the unnatural—unnatural as the Boom; and my recent experience parallels the wave of despair that swept the nation when the Boom was over.

I shall manage to live with the new dispensation, though it has taken some months to be certain of the fact. And just as the laughing stoicism which has enabled the American Negro to endure the intolerable conditions of his existence has cost him his sense of the truth—so in my case there is a price to pay. I do not any longer like the postman, nor the grocer, nor the editor, nor the cousin's husband, and he in turn will come to dislike me, so that life will never be very pleasant again, and the sign *Cave Canem* is hung permanently just above my door. I will try to be a correct animal though, and if you throw me a bone with enough meat on it I may even lick your hand.

EARLY SUCCESS

EARLY SUCCESS

October, 1937

Sᴇᴠᴇɴᴛᴇᴇɴ years ago this month I quit work or, if you pre-
fer, I retired from business. I was through—let the Street
Railway Advertising Company carry along under its own
power. I retired, not on my profits, but on my liabilities,
which included debts, despair, and a broken engagement
and crept home to St. Paul to "finish a novel."

That novel, begun in a training camp late in the war, was
my ace in the hole. I had put it aside when I got a job in
New York, but I was as constantly aware of it as of the shoe
with cardboard in the sole, during all one desolate spring. It
was like the fox and goose and the bag of beans. If I stopped
working to finish the novel, I lost the girl.

So I struggled on in a business I detested and all the confidence I had garnered at Princeton and in a haughty career
as the army's worst aide-de-camp melted gradually away.
Lost and forgotten, I walked quickly from certain places—
from the pawn shop where one left the field glasses, from
prosperous friends whom one met when wearing the suit

from before the war—from restaurants after tipping with the last nickel, from busy cheerful offices that were saving the jobs for their own boys from the war.

Even having a first story accepted had not proved very exciting. Dutch Mount and I sat across from each other in a car-card slogan advertising office, and the same mail brought each of us an acceptance from the same magazine—the old *Smart Set*.

"My check was thirty—how much was yours?"

"Thirty-five."

The real blight, however, was that my story had been written in college two years before, and a dozen new ones hadn't even drawn a personal letter. The implication was that I was on the down-grade at twenty-two. I spent the thirty dollars on a magenta feather fan for a girl in Alabama.

My friends who were not in love or who had waiting arrangements with "sensible" girls, braced themselves patiently for a long pull. Not I—I was in love with a whirl-wind and I must spin a net big enough to catch it out of my head, a head full of trickling nickels and sliding dimes, the incessant music box of the poor. It couldn't be done like that, so when the girl threw me over I went home and finished my novel. And then, suddenly, everything changed, and this article is about that first wild wind of success and the delicious mist it brings with it. It is a short and precious time—for when the mist rises in a few weeks, or a few months, one finds that the very best is over.

It began to happen in the autumn of 1919 when I was an empty bucket, so mentally blunted with the summer's writing that I'd taken a job repairing car roofs at the Northern Pacific shops. Then the postman rang, and that day I quit work and ran along the streets, stopping automobiles to tell friends and acquaintances about it—my novel *This Side of Paradise* was accepted for publication. That week the postman rang and rang, and I paid off my terrible small debts, bought a suit, and woke up every morning with a world of ineffable toploftiness and promise.

While I waited for the novel to appear, the metamorphosis of amateur into professional began to take place—a sort of stitching together of your whole life into a pattern of work, so that the end of one job is automatically the beginning of another. I had been an amateur before; in October, when I strolled with a girl among the stones of a southern graveyard, I was a professional and my enchantment with certain things that she felt and said was already paced by an anxiety to set them down in a story—it was called *The Ice Palace* and it was published later. Similarly, during Christmas week in St. Paul, there was a night when I had stayed home from two dances to work on a story. Three friends called up during the evening to tell me I had missed some rare doings: a well-known man-about-town had disguised himself as a camel and, with a taxi-driver as the rear half, managed to attend the wrong party. Aghast with myself for not being there, I spent the next day trying to collect the fragments of the story.

"Well, all I can say is it was funny when it happened." "No, I don't know where he got the taxi-man." "You'd have to know him well to understand how funny it was."

In despair I said:

"Well, I can't seem to find out exactly what happened but I'm going to write about it as if it was ten times funnier than anything you've said." So I wrote it, in twenty-two consecutive hours, and wrote it "funny," simply because I was so emphatically told it was funny. *The Camel's Back* was published and still crops up in the humorous anthologies.

With the end of the winter set in another pleasant pumped-dry period, and, while I took a little time off, a fresh picture of life in America began to form before my eyes. The uncertainties of 1919 were over—there seemed little doubt about what was going to happen—America was going on the greatest, gaudiest spree in history and there was going to be plenty to tell about it. The whole golden boom was in the air—its splendid generosities, its outrageous corruptions and the tortuous death struggle of the old America in prohibition. All the stories that came into my head had a touch of disaster in them—the lovely young creatures in my novels went to ruin, the diamond mountains of my short stories blew up, my millionaires were as beautiful and damned as Thomas Hardy's peasants. In life these things hadn't happened yet, but I was pretty sure living wasn't the reckless, careless business these people thought—this generation just younger than me.

For my point of vantage was the dividing line between the two generations, and there I sat—somewhat self-consciously. When my first big mail came in—hundreds and hundreds of letters on a story about a girl who bobbed her hair—it seemed rather absurd that they should come to me about it. On the other hand, for a shy man it was nice to be somebody except oneself again: to be "the Author" as one had been "the Lieutenant." Of course one wasn't really an author any more than one had been an army officer, but nobody seemed to guess behind the false face.

All in three days I got married and the presses were pounding out *This Side of Paradise* like they pound out extras in the movies.

With its publication I had reached a stage of manic

depressive insanity. Rage and bliss alternated hour by hour. A lot of people thought it was a fake, and perhaps it was, and a lot of others thought it was a lie, which it was not. In a daze I gave out an interview—I told what a great writer I was and how I'd achieved the heights. Heywood Broun, who was on my trail, simply quoted it with the comment that I seemed to be a very self-satisfied young man, and for some days I was notably poor company. I invited him to lunch and in a kindly way told him that it was too bad he had let his life slide away without accomplishing anything. He had just turned thirty and it was about then that I wrote a line which certain people will not let me forget: "She was a faded but still lovely woman of twenty-seven."

In a daze I told the Scribner Company that I didn't expect my novel to sell more than twenty thousand copies and when the laughter died away I was told that a sale of five thousand was excellent for a first novel. I think it was a week after publication that it passed the twenty thousand mark, but I took myself so seriously that I didn't even think it was funny.

These weeks in the clouds ended abruptly a week later when Princeton turned on the book—not undergraduate Princeton but the black mass of faculty and alumni. There was a kind but reproachful letter from President Hibben, and a room full of classmates who suddenly turned on me with condemnation. We had been part of a rather gay party staged conspicuously in Harvey Firestone's car of robin's-egg blue, and in the course of it I got an accidental black eye trying to stop a fight. This was magnified into an orgy and in spite of a delegation of undergraduates who went to the board of Governors, I was suspended from my club for a couple of months. The *Alumni Weekly* got after my book and only Dean Gauss had a good word to say for me. The unctuousness and hypocrisy of the proceedings was exasperating and for seven years I didn't go to Princeton. Then a magazine asked me for an article about it and when I started to write it, I found I really loved the place and that the experience of one week was a small item in the total budget. But on that day in 1920 most of the joy went out of my success.

But one was now a professional—and the new world couldn't possibly be presented without bumping the old out of the way. One gradually developed a protective hardness against both praise and blame. Too often people liked your things for the wrong reasons or people liked them whose dislike would be a compliment. No decent career was ever founded on a public and one learned to go ahead without precedents and without fear. Counting the bag, I found that in 1919 I had made $800 by writing, that in 1920 I had made $18,000, stories, picture rights and book. My story price had gone from $30 to $1,000. That's a small price to what was paid later in the Boom, but what it sounded like to me couldn't be exaggerated.

The dream had been early realized and the realization carried with it a certain bonus and a certain burden. Premature success gives one an almost mystical conception of destiny as opposed to will power—at its worst the Napoleonic delusion. The man who arrives young believes that he exercises his will because his star is shining. The man who only asserts himself at thirty has a balanced idea of what will power and fate have each contributed, the one who gets there at forty is liable to put the emphasis on will alone. This comes out when the storms strike your craft.

The compensation of a very early success is a conviction

that life is a romantic matter. In the best sense one stays young. When the primary objects of love and money could be taken for granted and a shaky eminence had lost its fascination, I had fair years to waste, years that I can't honestly regret, in seeking the eternal Carnival by the Sea. Once in the middle twenties I was driving along the High Corniche Road through the twilight with the whole French Riviera twinkling on the sea below. As far ahead as I could see was Monte Carlo, and though it was out of season and there were no Grand Dukes left to gamble and E. Phillips Oppenheim was a fat industrious man in my hotel, who lived in a bathrobe—the very name was so incorrigibly enchanting that I could only stop the car and like the Chinese whisper: "Ah me! Ah me!" It was not Monte Carlo I was looking at. It was back into the mind of the young man with cardboard soles who had walked the streets of New York. I was him again—for an instant I had the good fortune to share his dreams, I who had no more dreams of my own. And there are still times when I creep up on him, surprise him on an autumn morning in New York or a spring night in Carolina when it is so quiet that you can hear a dog barking in the next county. But never again as during that all too short period when he and I were one person, when the fulfilled future and the wistful past were mingled in a single gorgeous moment—when life was literally a dream.